Julius Lester won a Newbery Honor for his groundbreaking book, *To Be a Slave* (Dial). He is the critically acclaimed author of many books for children and adults, including *The Tales of Uncle Remus: The Adventures of Brer Rabbit*, illustrated by Jerry Pinkney, which was a winner of the Coretta Scott King Honor Award and an ALA Notable Book, and *Long Journey Home: Stories from Black History*, which was a National Book Award finalist.

Jerry Pinkney has been illustrating children's books for more than thirty-five years and has received three Caldecott Honors, for *John Henry*, *The Talking Eggs* by Robert D. San Souci, and *Mirandy and Brother Wind* by Patricia C. McKissack. *John Henry* was also an ALA Notable Book and an NCSS-CBC "Notable Children's Trade Book in the Field of Social Studies." Mr. Pinkney is an extremely successful artist whose work has been exhibited at the Art Institute of Chicago, the Schomburg Center for Black Culture in New York, and other museums.

JOHN HENRY

by JULIUS LESTER

pictures by JERRY PINKNEY

PUFFIN BOOKS

In memory of my father, James H., my John Henry.

J.P.

There are countless historical personages who do not engage us. Yet John Henry continues to move us by his affirmation of something triumphant which we hope is in all of us. After Phyllis Fogelman approached me to write a text based on the John Henry legend that Jerry Pinkney was researching and planning to illustrate, I called Jerry and asked him what he saw in John Henry. Jerry responded by talking about the transcendent quality of John Henry's humanity. As he talked, the image of Martin Luther King Jr. came to me, and it was then I knew I wanted to do the book.

This retelling is the result of the coming together of the creative spirits of Jerry Pinkney, those from whose lives came the song "John Henry," and myself. I'm still not certain what the connection is between John Henry and King. However, I suspect it is the connection all of us feel to both figures—namely, to have the courage to hammer until our hearts break and to leave our mourners smiling in their tears.

J.L.

PUFFIN BOOKS
Published by the Penguin Group
Penguin Putnam Books for Young Readers, 345 Hudson Street, New York, New York 10014, U.S.A.
Penguin Books Ltd, 27 Wrights Lane, London W8 5TZ, England
Penguin Books Australia Ltd, Ringwood, Victoria, Australia
Penguin Books Canada Ltd, 10 Alcorn Avenue, Toronto, Ontario, Canada M4V 3B2
Penguin Books (N.Z.) Ltd, 182-190 Wairau Road, Auckland 10, New Zealand

Penguin Books Ltd, Registered Offices: Harmondsworth, Middlesex, England

First published in the United States of America by Dial Books, a division of Penguin Books USA Inc., 1994
Published by Puffin Books, a member of Penguin Putnam Books for Young Readers, 1999

35 37 39 40 38 36 34

THE LIBRARY OF CONGRESS HAS CATALOGED THE DIAL EDITION AS FOLLOWS:
Lester, Julius.
John Henry / by Julius Lester
pictures by Jerry Pinkney.
p. cm.
Summary / Retells the life of the legendary African-American hero who raced
against a steam drill to cut through a mountain.
ISBN 0-8037-1606-0 (trade). ISBN 0-8037-1607-9 (lib. bdg.)
1. John Henry (Legendary character)—Legends. [1. John Henry (Legendary character).
2. Folklore, Afro-American. 3. Folklore—United States.] I. Pinkney, Jerry, ill. II. Title.
PZ8.1.L434Jo 1994 398.21—dc20 [E] 93-34583 CIP AC

Puffin Books ISBN 978-0-14-056622-2

Printed in the United States of America

The full-color artwork was prepared using pencil, colored pencils, and watercolor.

This tale attempts to be faithful to the indomitable human spirit John Henry embodies. It is this which makes questions of his historicity academically interesting, but finally secondary. Whether there was ever an actual person named John Henry is not certain. Numerous people believe in his actual existence, and numerous people have tried to prove it. Guy B. Johnson in his *John Henry: Tracking Down a Negro Legend* (1929) and L.W. Chappell in his *John Henry* (1933) each sought to establish the historicity of John Henry. Relying on testimony some fifty years after John Henry allegedly lived did not produce consistently convincing evidence. However, the figure of John Henry achieved his place in Americana through a novel, *John Henry* (1931) by Roark Bradford.

What is certain is that between 1870–1873 the Big Bend Tunnel on the Chesapeake & Ohio Railroad was built in the Allegheny Mountains in Summers County, West Virginia. This is the site of the Black folk ballad "John Henry," on which this text is based. There was probably an ex-slave named John Henry among those who worked on the tunnel, though there is little evidence of a contest between him and a steam drill.

There are many versions of the song, whose origin is unknown. Julius Lester relied on the ones in B.A. Botkin's *A Treasury of American Folklore* (1944), Alan Lomax's *Folk Songs of North America* (1960), and his own memory and experience as a former folk singer. In neither Botkin nor Lomax is it mentioned that John Henry was buried at the White House, but this is what Mr. Lester sang in the versions he performed. Where he heard that particular stanza or from what book he may have taken it, he does not remember. The present text is faithful to the ballad in the broad descriptions of the contest between John Henry and the steam drill. Lines directly from the versions of the songs mentioned above have also been used.

You have probably never heard of John Henry. Or maybe you heard about him but don't know the ins and outs of his comings and goings. Well, that's why I'm going to tell you about him.

When John Henry was born, birds came from everywhere to see him. The bears and panthers and moose and deer and rabbits and squirrels and even a unicorn came out of the woods to see him. And instead of the sun tending to his business and going to bed, it was peeping out from behind the moon's skirts trying to get a glimpse of the new baby.

Before long the mama and papa come out on the porch to show off their brand-new baby. The birds "oooooohed" and the animals "aaaaaahed" at how handsome the baby was.

Somewhere in the middle of one of the "oooooohs," or maybe it was on the backside of one of the "aaaaaaahs," that baby jumped out of his mama's arms and started growing.

He grew and he grew and he grew. He grew until his head and shoulders busted through the roof which was over the porch. John Henry thought that was the funniest thing in the world. He laughed so loud, the sun got scared. It scurried from behind the moon's skirts and went to bed, which is where it should've been all the while.

The next morning John Henry was up at sunrise. The sun wasn't. He was tired and had decided to sleep in. John Henry wasn't going to have none of that. He hollered up into the sky, "Get up from there! I got things to do and I need light to do 'em by."

The sun yawned, washed its face, flossed and brushed its teeth, and hurried up over the horizon.

That day John Henry helped his papa rebuild the porch he had busted through, added a wing onto the house with an indoor swimming pool and one of them jacutzis. After lunch he chopped down an acre of trees and split them into fireplace logs and still had time for a nap before supper.

The next day John Henry went to town. He met up with the meanest man in the state, Ferret-Faced Freddy, sitting on his big white horse. You know what he was doing? He was thinking of mean things to do. Ferret-Faced Freddy was so mean, he cried if he had a nice thought.

John Henry said, "Freddy, I'll make you a bet. Let's have a race. You on your horse. Me on my legs. If you and your horse win, you can work me as hard as you want for a whole year. If I win, you have to be nice for a year."

Ferret-Faced Freddy laughed an evil laugh. "It's a deal, John Henry." His voice sounded like bat wings on tombstones.

The next morning folks lined up all along the way the race
would go. John Henry was ready. Ferret-Faced Freddy and his
horse were ready.

BANG! The race was on.

My great-granddaddy's brother's cousin's sister-in-law's uncle's
aunt was there that morning. She said everybody saw Ferret-Faced
Freddy ride by on his big white horse and they were sho' 'nuf

moving. Didn't nobody see John Henry. That's because he was so fast, the wind was out of breath trying to keep up with him. When Ferret-Faced Freddy crossed the finish line, John Henry was already on the other side, sitting in a rocking chair and drinking a soda mom.

After that Ferret-Faced Freddy was so nice, everybody called him Frederick the Friendly.

John Henry decided it was time for him to go on down the big road. He went home and told his mama and daddy good-bye.

His daddy said, "You got to have something to make your way in the world with, Son. These belonged to your granddaddy." And he gave him two twenty-pound sledgehammers with four-foot handles made of whale bone.

A day or so later, John Henry saw a crew building a road. At least, that's what they were doing until they came on a boulder right smack-dab where the road was supposed to go. This was no ordinary boulder. It was as hard as anger and so big around, it took half a week for a tall man to walk from one side to the other.

John Henry offered to lend them a hand.

"That's all right. We'll put some dynamite to it."

John Henry smiled to himself. "Whatever you say."

The road crew planted dynamite all around the rock and set it off. KERBOOM BLAMMITY-BLAMMITY BOOMBOOM BANGBOOMBANG!!!

That dynamite made so much racket, the Almighty looked over the parapets of Heaven and hollered, "It's getting too noisy down there." The dynamite kicked up so much dirt and dust, it got dark. The moon thought night had caught her napping and she hurried out so fast, she almost bumped into the sun who was still climbing the steep hill toward noontime.

When all the commotion from the dynamite was over, the road crew was amazed. The boulder was still there. In fact, the dynamite hadn't knocked even a chip off it.

The crew didn't know what to do. Then they heard a rumbling noise. They looked around. It was John Henry, laughing. He said, "If you gentlemen would give me a little room, I got some work to do."

"Don't see how you can do what dynamite couldn't," said the boss of the crew.

John Henry chuckled. "Just watch me." He swung one of his hammers round and round his head. It made such a wind that leaves blew off the trees and birds fell out of the sky.

RINGGGGGG!

The hammer hit the boulder. That boulder shivered like you do on a cold winter morning when it looks like the school bus is never going to come.

RINGGGGGG!

The boulder shivered like the morning when freedom came to the slaves.

John Henry picked up his other hammer. He swung one hammer in a circle over his head. As soon as it hit the rock—RINGGGG!—the hammer in his left hand started to make a circle and—RINGGGG! Soon the RINGGGG! of one hammer followed the RINGGGG! of the other one so closely, it sounded like they were falling at the same time.

RINGGGG!RINGGGG!
RINGGGG!RINGGGG!

Chips and dust were flying from the boulder so fast that John Henry vanished from sight. But you could still hear his hammers—RINGGGG! RINGGGG!

The air seemed to be dancing to the rhythm of his hammers. The boss of the road crew looked up. His mouth dropped open. He pointed into the sky.

There, in the air above the boulder, was a rainbow. John Henry was swinging the hammers so fast, he was making a rainbow around his shoulders. It was shining and shimmering in the dust and grit like hope that never dies. John Henry started singing:

> I got a rainbow
> RINGGGG! RINGGGG!
> Tied round my shoulder
> RINGGGG! RINGGGG!
> It ain't gon' rain,
> No, it ain't gon' rain.
> RINGGGG! RINGGGG!

John Henry sang and he hammered and the air danced and the rainbow shimmered and the earth shook and rolled from the blows of the hammer. Finally it was quiet. Slowly the dust cleared.

Folks could not believe their eyes. The boulder was gone. In its place was the prettiest and straightest road they had ever seen. Not only had John Henry pulverized the boulder into pebbles, he had finished building the road.

In the distance where the new road connected to the main one, the road crew saw John Henry waving good-bye, a hammer on each shoulder, the rainbow draped around him like love.

John Henry went on his way. He had heard that any man good with a hammer could find work building the Chesapeake and Ohio Railroad through West Virginia. That was where he had been going when he stopped to build the road.

The next day John Henry arrived at the railroad. However, work had stopped. The railroad tracks had to go through a mountain, and such a mountain. Next to it even John Henry felt small.

But a worker told John Henry about a new machine they were going to use to tunnel through the mountain. It was called a steam drill. "It can hammer faster and harder than ten men and it never has to stop and rest."

The next day the boss arrived with the steam drill. John Henry said to him, "Let's have a contest. Your steam drill against me and my hammers."

The man laughed. "I've heard you're the best there ever was, John Henry. But even you can't outhammer a machine."

"Let's find out," John Henry answered.

Boss shrugged. "Don't make me no never mind. You start on the other side of the mountain. I'll start the steam drill over here. Whoever gets to the middle first is the winner."

The next morning all was still. The birds weren't singing and the roosters weren't crowing. When the sun didn't hear the rooster, he wondered if something was wrong. So he rose a couple of minutes early to see.

What he saw was a mountain as big as hurt feelings. On one side was a big machine hooked up to hoses. It was belching smoke and steam. As the machine attacked the mountain, rocks and dirt and underbrush flew into the air. On the other side was John Henry. Next to the mountain he didn't look much bigger than a wish that wasn't going to come true.

He had a twenty-pound hammer in each hand and muscles hard as wisdom in each arm. As he swung them through the air, they shone like silver, and when the hammers hit the rock, they rang like gold. Before long, tongues of fire leaped out with each blow.

On the other side the boss of the steam drill felt the mountain shudder. He got scared and hollered, "I believe this mountain is caving in!"

From the darkness inside the mountain came a deep voice: "It's just my hammers sucking wind. Just my hammers sucking wind." There wasn't enough room inside the tunnel for the rainbow, so it wrapped itself around the mountain on the side where John Henry was.

All through the night John Henry and the steam drill went at it. In the light from the tongues of fire shooting out of the tunnel from John Henry's hammer blows, folks could see the rainbow wrapped around the mountain like a shawl.

The sun came up extra early the next morning to see who

was winning. Just as it did, John Henry broke through and met
the steam drill. The boss of the steam drill was flabbergasted.
John Henry had come a mile and a quarter. The steam drill had
only come a quarter.

Folks were cheering and yelling, "John Henry! John Henry!"

John Henry walked out of the tunnel into the sunlight, raised his arms over his head, a hammer in each hand. The rainbow slid off the mountain and around his shoulders.

With a smile John Henry's eyes closed, and slowly he fell to the ground. John Henry was dead. He had hammered so hard and so fast and so long that his big heart had burst.

Everybody was silent for a minute. Then came the sound of soft crying. Some said it came from the moon. Another one said she saw the sun shed a tear.

Then something strange happened. Afterward folks swore the rainbow whispered it. I don't know. But whether it was a whisper or a thought, everyone had the same knowing at the same moment: "Dying ain't important. Everybody does that. What matters is how well you do your living."

First one person started clapping. Then another, and another. Soon everybody was clapping.

The next morning the sun got everybody up early to say good-bye to John Henry. They put him on a flatbed railroad car, and the train made its way slowly out of the mountains. All along the way folks lined both sides of the track, and they were cheering and shouting through their tears:

"John Henry! John Henry!"

John Henry's body was taken to Washington, D.C.

Some say he was buried on the White House lawn late one night while the President and the Mrs. President was asleep.

I don't know about none of that. What I do know is this: If you walk by the White House late at night, stand real still, and listen real closely, folks say you just might hear a deep voice singing:

I got a rainbow
RINGGGG! RINGGGG!
Tied round my shoulder
RINGGGG! RINGGGG!
It ain't gon' rain,
No, it ain't gon' rain.
RINGGGG! RINGGGG!